beetle bailey ®

BY MORT WALKER

LIFE'S A BEACH!

The cartoons in this volume
also appear in the Giant Size
BEETLE BAILEY:
RISE AND SHINE

D0642919

TOR

A TOM DOHERTY ASSOCIATES BOOK

This is a work of fiction. All the characters and events portrayed in this book are fictional, and any resemblance to real people or incidents is purely coincidental.

BEETLE BAILEY: LIFE'S A BEACH

Copyright © 1987 by King Features Syndicate, Inc.

The cartoons in this volume also appear in the Giant Size BEETLE BAILEY: RISE AND SHINE

All rights reserved, including the right to reproduce this book or portions thereof in any form.

First Tor printing: January 1987

A TOR Book

Published by Tom Doherty Associates, Inc.
49 West 24 Street
New York, N.Y. 10010

ISBN: 0-812-56117-1
CAN. ED.: 0-812-56118-X

Printed in the United States of America

0 9 8 7 6 5 4 3 2 1

© 1986 King Features Syndicate. Inc

Friendship

Friendship is a footbridge joining isolated bodies together allowing free and confident passage, sharing what each has, and adding to the sum total of each.

To be a friend one must be as tolerant to the other as to himself. thus the self is made larger and stronger. A good friend is one who will lend as though giving and repay more than is lent!

Cherish your friends... they make up a man's wealth more surely than gold... for a man without a friend is like a cork without a bottle.

© King Features Syndicate, Inc., 1977.

It is not necessary to tell a friend you like him. He knows. But tell him anyway. Friendship, like plants, blooms greater when nourished.

11-13

Defend your friends, elevate your friends, help your friends, and you will find even your enemies will want to be your friends.

I JUST WANTED YOU TO PAINT "FRIENDSHIP" ON THE SIDE OF MY VAN!

WELL...ONCE I GOT STARTED...

MORT WALKER

12-11 © King Features Syndicate, Inc., 1977. World rights reserved.

© King Features Syndicate, Inc., 1978. World rights reserved.

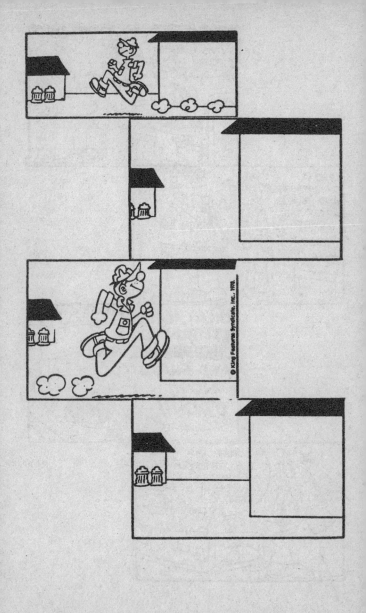

© King Features Syndicate, Inc., 1978.

7-2

© King Features Syndicate, Inc., 1978. World rights reserved.

© King Features Syndicate, Inc., 1978.

BEETLE BAILEY
THE WACKIEST G.I. IN THE ARMY

☐   49003-8   BEETLE BAILEY GIANT EDITION #1 $2.50
☐   49006-2   BEETLE BAILEY GIANT #2: HEY THERE! $2.50
☐   49007-0   BEETLE BAILEY GIANT #3:
      ROUGH RIDERS $2.50
☐   49008-9   BEETLE BAILEY GIANT #4:
      GENERAL ALERT $2.50
☐   49051-8   BEETLE BAILEY GIANT #5:
      RISE AND SHINE! $2.50

☐   56080-9   BEETLE BAILEY GIANT #6:
      DOUBLE TROUBLE $2.50
☐   56081-7   Canada $2.95

☐   56086-8   BEETLE BAILEY GIANT #7:
      YOU CRACK ME UP $2.50
☐   56087-6   Canada $2.95

☐   56092-2   BEETLE BAILEY GIANT #8:
      SURPRISE PACKAGE $2.50
☐   56093-0   Canada $2.95

☐   56098-1   BEETLE BAILEY GIANT #9:
      TOUGH LUCK $2.50
☐   56099-X   Canada $2.95

☐   56100-7   BEETLE BAILEY #10: REVENGE $2.50
☐   56101-5   Canada $2.95

Buy them at your local bookstore or use this handy coupon:
Clip and mail this page with your order

TOR BOOKS—Reader Service Dept.
49 W. 24 Street, 9th Floor, New York, NY 10010

Please send me the book(s) I have checked above. I am enclosing
$_____ (please add $1.00 to cover postage and handling).
Send check or money order only—no cash or C.O.D.'s.

Mr./Mrs./Miss _____

Address _____

City _____ State/Zip _____

Please allow six weeks for delivery. Prices subject to change without
notice.